Toby's Best Friend

Illustrated by Sophie Casson
Translated by Sarah Cummins

First Novels

Formac Publishing Company Limited
Halifax, Nova Scotia

Originally published as *Le bonheur est une tempête avec un chien*
Copyright © 2002 Les éditions de la courte échelle inc
Translation copyright © 2003 Sarah Cummins

Formac Publishing Company Limited acknowledges the support of the Cultural Affairs Section, Nova Scotia Department of Tourism and Culture. We acknowledge the financial support of the Government of Canada through the Book Publishing Industry Development Program (BPIDP) for our publishing activities.

We acknowledge the support of the Canada Council for the Arts for our publishing program.

National Library of Canada Cataloguing in Publication Data

Lemieux, Jean, 1954-
[Bonheur est une tempête avec un chien. English]
    Toby's best friend / by Jean Lemieux ; illustrated by Sophie Casson.

(First novels ; 47)
Translation of: Le bonheur est une tempête avec un chien.
ISBN 0-88780-611-2 (bound).—ISBN 0-88780-610-4 (pbk.)

    I. Casson, Sophie II. Title. III. Title: Bonheur est une tempête avec un chien. English. IV. Series.

PS8573.E5427B6613 2003   jC843'.54   C2003-903921-8

Formac Publishing Company Ltd.
5502 Atlantic Street
Halifax, Nova Scotia, B3H 1G4
www.formac.ca

Printed and bound in Canada

Distributed in the United States by:
Orca Book Publishers
P.O. Box 468 Custer, WA
USA 98240-0468

Distributed in the UK by:
Roundabout Books (a division of Roundhouse Publishing Ltd.)
31 Oakdale Glen, Harrogate,
N Yorkshire, HG1 2YJ

Table of Contents

1
For My Own Good

I think I asked one too many questions again today. When I got home from school, my mom was in the kitchen watering her plants.

"Mom," I asked her. "Will the Earth die before I do or after?"

She gave me a worried look. She explained that the Earth was not going to die, not for hundreds and thousands of years. Of course, we have to take good care of the Earth. But it would last for all my life, so there was nothing to worry about. The Earth would be there for me, with its forests and

animals and oceans.

"But what about pollution?" I objected. "And new clear warheads?"

Mom put down her watering can. She sat down and took me on her lap. I like that. Mom's arms are softer than the fur of my friend Beebee's cat. And Mom smells good.

"Nu-cle-ar warheads," she corrected me. "Toby, you seem to be suffering from anxiety."

We had talked about this before. Anxiety is like being afraid, only you don't really know what you're afraid of. Your hands are all shaky and you feel like there's a big hole in your chest.

When you suffer from

anxiety, you always have questions, just like I do. Why doesn't *cough* rhyme with *though?* Why does every dog have its day, but not every cat? What comes after the very last number?

Mom thought that anxiety is not good for my health. She had a very serious look on her face.

"We'll have to do something about this, Toby," she said. "For your own good."

* * *

After dinner, Mom asked Dad to walk to the park with her. I was suspicious. I know my parents. Whenever they have a problem to settle, they go for a walk.

I went down to the basement. My brother Will was down there, practising his slapshot with a tennis ball.

"Will, Mom is planning to do something for my own good."

Will is eleven years old. He's athletic. He's bigger than I am, and stronger. He doesn't have much to say. When he does speak, he talks ve-ry slow-ly, as if he was choosing each word from a treasure chest inside his head.

"YAH!" he said, and shot the ball into the upper left-hand corner of the net. Then he turned to me.

"Watch out," he advised me, in a serious tone.

He fetched the ball and got

ready to shoot again.

"Why?" I asked.

"The last time Mom and Dad decided to do something for my own good, they took the computer away for two weeks."

I remembered that time. Will likes hockey, skateboarding, and basketball. But above all, he loves computer games. Last spring, when he got a bad report card, Mom and Dad said no more computer.

"Will, what is *my own good*?"

He did a double fake, turned, and shot the ball into the net.

"Parents think they know what's best for us. When they say, 'It's for your own good,' that means they're about to force something on you."

2
Seeing a Specialist

As I went back upstairs, I thought over what Will had said.

He was right! Every time my parents say, "It's for your own good," they force something on me! Eat your vegetables, for your own good. Time to go to bed, for your own good. Do your homework, for your own good.

I was beginning to think that *good* is whatever parents decide their kids should do. It's not fair.

While I was thinking, the snow had been falling, and my parents still hadn't come back. It was the first big snowfall of the year! I had been waiting for ages to take my snowboard out.

I thought some more. Maybe there was no such thing as *good.* I went to look in the dictionary.

Good: what is beneficial or morally right

What does *beneficial* mean? I know what *right* means, but what about *morally right*?

When Mom and Dad got back, their cheeks were glowing from the cold and their eyes were sparkling.

"We're going for a little ride," Dad announced.

"Can I come?"

"Not this time, Toby. We'll be back in about an hour."

They drove off in the van,

like thieves in the night. I would have liked to discuss with them what morally right was, but it would have to wait.

I sat down on the couch in the living room. I knew Mom and Dad were cooking up something. What could it be?

I turned on the TV. There was nothing good on. Even the cartoons didn't interest me. A whole hour to wait and worry!

Maybe they were going to send me to boarding school. Or to a psychologist. Or make me swallow some disgusting medicine.

The minutes dragged on. Will and my sister Emily came in and sat down in front of the TV with me. What would

Emily say if I snuggled up next to her, like I used to do when I was little?

I didn't have a chance to try it out because just then I heard the car pulling in and the doors slamming.

Dad came in, his glasses all fogged up. He looked serious as he turned off the TV and wiped his glasses on his shirt.

"Children, your mother and I have made an important decision. Things have to change at home. Especially with Toby and all his questions."

Dad's eyes rested on me. But where was Mom?

"We have decided we need a specialist. An anti-anxiety expert. Marie!" he called out.

Mom came in, pulling
something on the end of a rope.
It was a dog!

3
What's His Name?

For months, for years, ever since the day I was born and even before, I had wanted to have a dog. Any dog, as long as it had four paws and said *woof! woof!* and would play with me.

My parents had always said no. It was a big responsibility to have a dog. I promised that I would take care of it and feed it and vacuum up its hair and clean up its messes.

But it didn't make any difference. Mom and Dad didn't believe I would do it. They said I could get a dog later, when I had left home.

So, now, I couldn't believe that I had a real dog of my very own! The dog walked into the living room, its tongue hanging out. It sat down and looked at us with its big, shiny eyes.

"Is it a boy or a girl?" asked Emily.

"A boy," said Dad.

"I would have preferred a girl," she grumped. "There are already three guys in the house."

I looked at my new friend. He wasn't very handsome.

He was of average size, not big and not little. His fur was not short and not long, and it hung over his eyes. His ears stuck out like airplane wings. He had black, white, and brown spots, all mixed up.

I had said I would take any old dog, and any old dog was what I got.

My dad likes inventions and scientists. The dog he chose looked like an experiment. One thing was certain: this dog was like no other dog I had ever seen, in real life or in books.

"What breed of dog is he?" I asked.

Dad put his glasses back on and examined the dog, but he couldn't tell its breed.

"It's a…a terrier," Mom ventured. "A Neapolitan terrier. Mixed, like Neapolitan ice cream, not really a Neapolitan from Naples," she explained.

I suggested we call him

Naples. Emily burst out laughing.

"Naples is a place in Italy! That's no name for a dog."

"Why can't it be a dog's name?" I was cross.

Emily just shrugged. Same old thing — I was too young to understand! Mom winked at me. That was her way of asking me to be reasonable.

Why should I, Toby Omeranovic, age eight, be expected to be more reasonable than my sister, who's fourteen?

I know the answer. It's because Emily is a teenager.

It must be great to be a teenager. You can be as cheerful and charming as a fire hydrant. You can sleep until two in the

afternoon. You can dye your hair
purple or green. You can tell
your little brother that Naples is
no name for a dog.

You can do all of that, and your parents won't turn a hair. Mom explained the other day that adolescence is like a storm or a blackout. You just have to wait until it's over.

When she's around eighteen, Emily will return to normal. In the meantime, we still had to find a name for the dog.

"How about Napoleon?" suggested Will.

Silence.

"Napoleon's a great name. And it sounds like Naples and Neapolitan."

Nobody was against it. Wagging his tail, Napoleon watched as Mom gave him his first bowl of dog food.

"Napoleon suits him," said

Emily approvingly.

"Who was Napoleon?" I wondered.

"He was an emperor," said Dad.

"What's an emperor?"

"Like a great king."

I went over to my new friend and stroked his three-coloured fur. Napoleon. He might not be handsome, but he had the name of an emperor.

If this was how my parents wanted to look out for my own good, I had no objection.

4
Napoleon in the Basement

Anxiety is great. Thanks to my anxiety, Napoleon belongs a bit more to me than to the others.

You have to take dogs out at least twice a day so they can get fresh air and do their business. Napoleon took his first walk with Dad and me.

We walked down the street. It was snowing again, fat flakes that stuck to the trees instead of falling to the ground and turning into slush.

Napoleon was excited. He pulled on his leash and peed against every pole we passed.

"What does *morally right* mean, Dad?"

"Ask Napoleon. He's the expert."

"Dad! At your age, you should know that dogs don't answer questions."

He was silent. I figured he wanted to just walk without having to think hard.

"You and Mom always say, 'It's for your own good.' What's *my good?*"

Dad tried to scratch his head, but that's pretty hard with gloves and a toque on.

"*Good* is what makes people happy," he answered. "It can be a lot of different things. It's something different for each person."

"There's not just one good?"
"Of course not!"
Somehow, I didn't think I
understood any better.

* * *

When we got home, Emily and
Will took Napoleon. They
petted him and stroked him and
showed him around the house.

I had a plan. I spread a
blanket on the floor by my bed.
Next to it I placed a dish of food
and a bowl of water. That night
I would have something more
than the nightlight to keep me
company.

"Hop into bed now, Toby!"
Mom said when she came to
tuck me in.

Then she noticed the blanket.

"The dog cannot spend the night in your room, Toby. Napoleon will sleep in the basement."

In the basement! He would be so lonely!

I argued, I protested, but it did no good. Mom wouldn't budge.

"Napoleon has to get used to his new home. He mustn't be spoiled. It's for his own good!"

His own good! I nearly flipped.

"No more arguments, Toby!" Mom gently scolded me. "Napoleon is sleeping in the basement, and that's final."

She turned on the nightlight and left, wagging her finger at me.

I lay in bed, stewing.

Mom was so mean! I could hear Napoleon barking downstairs. He sounded unhappy. But Dad had said that *good* made people happy!

I shook with rage. What was the point of having a dog if he couldn't even be with me? I could hear muffled whimpers from the basement. Napoleon was crying…

I vowed to rescue him.

5
Too Much Love

I was so angry that it was easy to stay awake. To help pass the time, I read the encyclopedia.

Napoleon Bonaparte was quite a character. He wore a funny cocked hat with two corners and he always held his right hand inside his jacket, as if he had a stomach ache. His wife was named Josephine.

Napoleon conquered lots of countries in Europe. He led his Grand Army to the pyramids of Egypt and declared himself emperor.

He also made a lot of

enemies, so many that he lost a
battle against the English and
the Prussians at Waterloo.
Prussians are a kind of
Germans, with moustaches.

Napoleon died all alone, on
an island.

I looked at one of the illus-
trations, showing Napoleon's

Grand Army fighting the enemy. It was no picnic. Soldiers were shooting and stabbing one another. They were being hit by cannon balls and pierced by bayonets. There was blood everywhere.

Did Napoleon think he was fighting the English for their own good?

It was like the news on TV. Fighting, famine, war…how could you understand it? It was the good of some people against the good of others.

I decided to consult my specialist.

* * *

Will and Emily went up to bed,

followed a little later by my
parents. I heard them talking for
a while, then the house was
silent.

I got out of bed and put on
my slippers. I tiptoed down the
hall past my parents' bedroom. I
could hear my dad snoring.

Perfect. I crept downstairs,
taking care to not make the fifth
step creak. In the kitchen, the

light on the stove cast a moonlit glow.

Outside, it was snowing harder. I heard Napoleon whimper. He must have heard me. I went down to the basement and found him lying next to the lawn mower.

He wagged his tail excitedly and barked twice. I held my finger to my lips. *Shh!*

He understood. I picked him up and took him upstairs. He headed straight for his bowl. Always hungry! I fed him and then made myself a Toby Special: a peanut-butter-jam-and-banana sandwich.

We sat in front of the big window in the living room. Happiness is a snowstorm and a puppy. Outside, the snowplows were hard at work piling up the snow on one side of the street.

A gigantic snowbank was growing in front of Beebee's house. (Beebee's real name is Catherine Bainbridge-Babcock, but we call her Beebee for short.)

"See, Napoleon? Tomorrow we can build a fort."

Napoleon yapped in approval. He panted and stared at me with his big eyes. What a friend!

"You know, Napoleon, I am pretty tired of being a kid. My

parents decide everything for me. It's supposed to be for my own good."

I sighed. Napoleon watched the snowplows.

"Sometimes, I wish I didn't have any good. Then they would leave me alone."

I heard someone cough behind me. My mom was sitting on the steps, in her dressing gown.

"So you wish I would just leave you alone?" she asked.

Napoleon! Do something! Don't just sit there like a rutabaga!

Mom came and sat cross-legged behind me. She lifted me onto her lap.

"Your Dad and I do things for

your own good because we love you."

"Do you think you could love me a little less?"

Mom kissed my hair.

"Impossible! We will love you lots and lots your whole life long."

What did I tell you, Napoleon? Parents are worse than adolescence. At least there's an end to adolescence.

6
Fort Napoleon

Mom said she loves me, but she still wouldn't let Napoleon sleep in my room. Sometimes parents just stick to their guns, even when they know they're wrong.

They call that authority.

There's nothing I can do about it. I'm only eight years old. I don't have a driver's licence. I don't have money to buy food at the supermarket. I have to stay at home until I grow up. Afterwards, I can go live in an apartment, like Beebee's older sister, and do whatever I want.

I went back to bed with a heavy heart. It took me a long time to fall asleep.

In the morning, when I pulled up the shade, the snow was blowing from right to left. The wind had come up during the night.

I went down to the kitchen. Dad was eating his breakfast and reading the paper. Napoleon was lying at Dad's feet with his tongue hanging out, hoping for a few scraps to fall.

"Dad, is this a blizzard?"

When there's a blizzard, the schools close.

"I think so. See what they say on the radio."

Great! I ate my cereal in the living room, still wearing my

pyjamas. I kept my eyes on the cartoons and my ears on the radio. Finally they announced that my school was closed.

I felt really lucky! A blizzard and a dog, at the same time! I looked outside. The mountain in front of the Bainbridge-Babcocks' house had grown taller still.

I called Marianne, Sigi, and Beebee. Half an hour later, they appeared at my front door, carrying a shovel.

"Let me introduce you to Napoleon!"

They were very impressed. They had never seen a dog like him before. I told them that Neapolitan terriers were a very rare breed.

They thought Napoleon was a great name.

"It's the name of an emperor," I explained.

They nodded. I went to get dressed. Then we all went outside with Napoleon.

It wasn't too cold and the wind was dying down. The mountain of snow was higher than a truck. I climbed up to the top.

"Today, we are going to build the biggest fort ever," I shouted.

"Not just a fort — a fortress! We will call it Fort Napoleon!"

We set to work. Napoleon was not very helpful. He just chased cars, nibbled on our boots, and barked at the sparrows perched on the power lines.

"Maybe Napoleon could help pull the blocks of snow," suggested Beebee.

We tied him to my sled, but he just lay down in the snow and looked at us and panted.

"Napoleon is lazy," said Sigi.

"What shall we do with him, when the fort is finished?" asked Marianne, always practical.

I had an idea. "We'll build him a kennel!"

The mountaintop had been transformed into a castle strong enough to resist the worst enemy assaults. In one corner we dug a hole about a metre deep.

Then I ran home and fetched a bowl of dog food and my dad's old blue sweater. Napoleon hopped right into his hole, lay down on the sweater, and wolfed down his snack.

That was fine, then! For the final touch, we dug a tunnel behind the castle. It must have been three metres long. The entrance was hidden behind a huge snowball.

Snug in his little kennel, Napoleon had fallen asleep on the blue sweater.

My friends and I surveyed our work. We were tired and hungry, but we had built Fort Napoleon.

"The only thing missing is the enemy attackers," observed Marianne.

Sigi tapped me on the shoulder. Her hair blowing in the wind, a scarf tied around her throat, my mother was advancing full-steam ahead.

7
A Near-catastrophe

"Mom! Mom! Come see our fort!"

I ran to meet her, overjoyed at the chance to show her our work. She did not look pleased. She bent over me and looked me in the eye.

"Toby! Did you remember the snowplow rule?"

The snowplow rule? Then I remembered. You-must-never-build-a-snowfort-in-the-street-because-you-could-be-gobbled-up-by-the-snowplow.

"There's nothing to worry about, Mom. We'll hear the

snowplow if it comes."

She walked over to Fort Napoleon and then she saw the tunnel. She stuck her head inside. When she pulled it out again, she looked even less pleased than before.

"A tunnel, Toby! What did we tell you about tunnels?"

Suddenly, I wasn't in such a good mood myself.

"I know! Tunnels-are-dangerous-because-they-can-collapse-and-suffocate-the-children-inside!"

"You'll have to knock the tunnel down."

A wave of disappointment and anger swept over me. Marianne, Sigi, and Beebee watched from one side. I stood between Mom and the fortress.

"No!" I said, between clenched teeth.

"It's for your own good, Toby!"

My own good! I exploded.

"You mean *your* own good! You just say that to make me do what you want! I hate you!"

Mom stared at me, her eyes like two bazookas.

"What did you say?"

"I said I hate you! You are the worst mother on the face of the Earth!"

My mother is usually a gentle, affectionate person. She hardly ever loses her temper. But when she does, she turns into a tyrannosaurus.

Without warning, she grabbed

me by the scruff of the neck and dragged me away.

"So I'm the worst mother on the face of the Earth, am I?"

She turned back to my friends. "Time to go home for your lunch now, kids."

Marianne, Sigi, and Beebee walked off, their heads down. Before I knew what had happened, I was in my room.

"You can come out when you are ready to apologize!" Mom announced.

"Never! I won't take it back. You are the worst mother in the world!"

"Think about this, young man. You are eight years old. You are not old enough to decide what is best for yourself.

Until you are, your father and I will make the decisions."

"I do so know what's best for me!"

She shut the door. I threw myself on the bed and cried tears of rage.

Suddenly, I heard a rumbling in the street. Then warning sirens and the sounds of an engine.

It must be Mom's big bad snowplow. It was going past my window. It must have already demolished our fort.

Napoleon!

Napoleon was napping in the fort! I raced out of my room and tumbled down the stairs. Mom was in the living room.

"Mom…the dog…"

She turned as white as sugar, whiter than the snow. We grabbed our coats and rushed out.

To our left, the snow trucks and the plow were driving off, their destruction work complete. Where Fort Napoleon had once stood, there was nothing but the big snowball that had guarded the entrance to the tunnel.

"My dog! My poor dog!"

I burst into sobs. Napoleon was dead, and it was my fault!

Mom gathered me in her arms and tried her best to comfort me.

"It's not your fault, Toby. I should have remembered Napoleon, too. Maybe he managed to hide somewhere."

I couldn't stop crying. We

looked everywhere and called his name until we were hoarse, but there was not a trace of him. All we found were a few pieces of blue sweater, scattered on the snow.

Poor Napoleon! The snowplow had turned him into hamburger. I buried my face in my mother's side.

"I'm sorry, Mom. I should have listened to you."

Then I heard a familiar bark. I turned around. Napoleon was running out of the Bainbridge-Babcocks' house!

Napoleon jumped into my arms and I held him close. I was never so happy in my whole life!

Beebee followed Napoleon

out, her lips smeared with chocolate. After my quarrel with Mom she had noticed the snowplow at the end of the street, so she went to get Napoleon out of the fort. He was still sleeping. She took him to her house to meet her cat.

"You saved his life, Beebee."

She blushed. "It was nothing. I wish I had a dog, too."

I buried my face in Napoleon's fur. I'll take better care of you in future, my precious dog!

For your own good.

Three more new novels in the *First Novels Series*!

Leo's Poster Challenge
by Louise Leblanc

When Leo's teacher announces a poster contest, Leo sees a chance to win out over Butch, the class bully. Leo can submit a poster drawn by his talented vampire friend Julio. But Butch accuses Leo of cheating. Will Leo have to tell everyone about his secret friend Julio?

Maddie on TV
by Louise Leblanc

An excited Maddie tries out for a commercial with the stars of her favourite tv show. At the auditions, Maddie is downhearted when she sees all the people who want the part—including her classmate Clementine. To her surprise, Maddie is chosen—but other, less pleasant surprises follow.

Marilou Forecasts the Future
by Raymond Plante

When Marilou finds an astrologer's briefcase, she is rewarded with her own chart. Marilou decides to draw charts for her friends, and is soon making predictions for them and using clever tricks to see into the future. Her friend Boris isn't convinced—is it all really astrology?

Other Leo titles:

Leo and Julio

Other Maddie titles:

Maddie's Millionaire Dreams
Maddie Needs Her Own Life
Maddie Wants New Clothes
Maddie Tries to be Good
Maddie in Trouble
Maddie in Hospital
Maddie in Goal
Maddie in Danger
Maddie Goes to Paris
Maddie Wants Music
That's Enough Maddie

Other Marilou titles:

Marilou Cries Wolf
Marilou, Iguana Hunter
Marilou on Stage
Marilou's Long Nose

Formac Publishing Company Limited
5502 Atlantic Street, Halifax, Nova Scotia B3H 1G4
Orders: 1-800-565-1975 Fax: (902) 425-0166
www.formac.ca